For Sara and my mother

Second U.S. edition 1998

Library of Congress Cataloging-in-Publication Data

Lewis, Kim.
Emma's lamb / Kim Lewis.—2nd U.S. ed.
p.   cm.
Summary: Emma looks after a lost lamb, plays games with him,
and helps him find his mother.
ISBN 0-7636-0424-0
[1. Sheep—Fiction.] I. Title.
PZ7.L58723Em   1998
[E]—dc21   97-27248

2 4 6 8 10 9 7 5 3 1

Printed in Hong Kong

This book was typeset in Garamond.
The pictures were done in colored pencil.

CANDLEWICK PRESS
2067 Massachusetts Avenue
Cambridge, Massachusetts 02140

Emma's Lamb

Kim Lewis

One rainy spring morning at lambing time,
Emma's father put a little lost lamb in a box
by the stove. Then he went back
to the field to look for Lamb's mother.

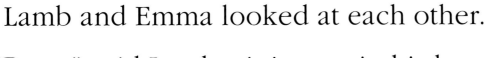Lamb and Emma looked at each other.

"Baaa," said Lamb, sitting up in his box.

Emma wanted to keep little Lamb
and look after him all by herself.

So Emma dried Lamb
because he was very wet.
She tried to keep him warm
because he was very cold.
Emma fed Lamb
because he was very hungry.

When Lamb was dry and warm and fed,

he and Emma played.

"Baaa," said Lamb.

Then Emma took Lamb for a walk
and he skipped along behind her.
Emma decided to play hide-and-seek.
She closed her eyes and counted to ten.
"Here I come!" she cried.

Emma looked for Lamb in the stable.

She looked for him in the barn.

She looked for him in the granary.

She looked all around the yard.

She couldn't find Lamb in the house.

He wasn't in his box.

She couldn't find him in the

sheep pens either.

"I give up!" she shouted.

But Lamb was nowhere to be found.

Emma didn't want to play anymore.

She wanted Lamb to come back.

She thought he might be cold and hungry.

"Where are you, Lamb?" she cried.

"Baaa," came a sound from the hay shed.

Emma ran inside to look.

Lamb sat up in the nesting box,

where the hens had laid their eggs.

"Baaa," he cried and ran to Emma.

"Lamb, I thought I'd lost you," said Emma,

holding him very tight.

She couldn't look after Lamb all by herself.

He needed to be with his mother.

But where was she?

Then Emma saw her father across the field.

A ewe without a lamb ran ahead of him, calling.

"Baaa," cried Lamb. He wriggled to get free.

Emma put him down,

and Lamb ran as fast as he could to his mother.

Emma went to the field the very next day.

When she called, Lamb came running to see her.

"Will you remember me when you're bigger?" asked Emma.

Lamb and Emma looked at each other.

"Baaa," said Lamb, waggling his tail.